ALSO BY ARI NEWMAN

Mrs. Vanderbilt

AMERICA FIRST

A Modern Fable

ARI NEWMAN

AMERICA FIRST A Modern Fable

All Rights Reserved
Copyright © 2017 Ari Newman
Edited by Dianne Z. Newman

A derivative work of the screenplay
STATE OF THE UNION Copyright © 2007 Ari Newman
The Library of Congress has catalogued the U.S. edition as follows:
Copyright Registration Number: PAu003078040
ISBN: 978-0-9986672-1-8

Published By
Mrs. Vanderbilt Novel LLC
First Edition Published 2017
WRITTEN IN JERUSALEM ISRAEL
PUBLISHED IN THE UNITES STATES OF AMERICA

To Mom and Dad,
I love you so much

CONTENTS

PREFACE

I began to convert my screenplay into a book on Sunday morning, January 22, 2017 after experiencing the events in Washington D.C. and around the world during the previous 48 hours. I originally planned to spend the day enjoying some NFL football.

The screenplay was originally written in 2006 after hearing the then unknown state senator Barack Obama say these words, "to slice-and-dice our country into Red States and Blue States; Red States for Republicans, Blue States for Democrats...there is not a liberal America and a conservative America — there is the United States of America. There is not a black America and a white America and Latino America and Asian America — there's the United States of America."

My partners and I were about to produce the film having received a preliminary green-light from the first studio that read it. We were assigned an account executive and everything was moving ahead until everything in Hollywood stopped due to the Writer's Guild strike. Within several weeks, the project's account executive along with thousands of others' jobs had been lost; it took years for the motion picture industry to recover while simultaneously experiencing a deflating DVD market and the Great Recession. Those who have enjoyed HBO's *Entourage* or have screened the films *The Player* or Kevin Bacon's *The Big Picture* realize that this type of scenario is very common in the motion picture business. Like everybody else, we moved on with other projects knowing that we could always pull it off the shelf. With Obama's presidency attempting to tackle the Red State / Blue State divide, the time wasn't right for this storyline.

Two final thoughts – Since this book was adapted from a screenplay it is written in a simple and easy to understand manner. While the story addresses complex issues related to government and politics (hopefully to be enjoyed by all regardless of political ideology) it is not filled with fancy wording or with the intention of being the best fable ever written. For this reason, it is perfect for younger readers (14 and up i.e. "PG-13") who might not be the best readers (I wasn't at that age) or for those where English is a second language to improve reading comprehension and/or to initiate discussion and healthy debate about government, American history, political science, etc. Finally, and for me perhaps the most important, I want to use this opportunity to thank everyone from near and far for their support and encouragement and for those who believed in me even when I didn't believe in myself.

Please feel welcome to post any comments or thoughts you may have about the book or any topic or theme political, literary, or whatever...

Dedicated to those who feel that they don't have a voice – you do and you are not alone.

Poet Danny Siegel teaches that when W.H. Auden was asked about the meaning of his poetry he said, "My poetry never saved a child from Auschwitz."

FORWARD

History repeats itself as we are again in danger of moving from terrorism to war, The Third Great War. The causes of the Second World War combined with the reasons the Central Powers lost World War I are precisely what has and is now happening.

Barbara Tuchman outlined how the stage was set for the Great War with the funeral of Edward VII and a conflict that began brewing among three cousins: the King, the Kaiser and the Tzar. The Schlieffen plan was doomed to fail not only because it was outdated, but once Germany found itself trapped in a trench warfare stalemate, the plan did not account for a war of attrition. Although the assassination of Archduke Franz Ferdinand triggered the honoring of alliance treaties which ultimately led to World War I, it was lost due to a flawed strategy, unachievable operational goals, and poor tactics.

The Second Great War became a question of "when" and not "if" when experts in war planning, personified by the fictitious character Pug Henry in Herman Wouk's "The Winds of War" challenged conventional wisdom by advising FDR that Poland would be next, after the German/Russian proxy war in Spain during its revolution, Japan's invasion of China, and most significant, Chamberlain's appeasement of Hitler after Germany annexed Austria and the Sudetenland. Subsequently, when Germany breached the Munich Agreement, a vacuum was created in Czechoslovakia allowing its neighbors to grab disputed territory. Pug Henry predicted that although Polish independence would be guaranteed by Britain and France, Hitler would not be deterred; then in September 1939, using the pretext of Polish aggression, Germany invaded Poland leading to World War II.

The stage was set for the Third Great War when American and its Western allies removed the Iraqi army from Kuwait. For the first time since the Versailles Treaty, the Allies put hundreds of thousands of troops on the ground to redraw and control the map of ancient Mesopotamia. Although Iraq was repelled, the Bush Plan created many more problems than it solved, and its ultimate failure led to two falling dominoes: First, in the Muslim world the Salafists, Wahhabis, and others gained legitimacy with groups like Al-Qaida, and second, a decade later Bush the Son, considered by many on the streets in the Arab world to be his father's heir, would invade Iraq using the false pretext that it was retaliation for the 911 attacks. While Baghdad quickly fell, the war was lost because Bush held an outdated view of the role of mass media and never took into account the importance of social media and all that it would reveal. Abu Ghraib, the failed policy of de-baathification, and the weapons of mass destruction fiasco all led to decreasing support for the war in America and amongst her Allies, attrition amongst the troops, and the deaths of hundreds of thousands of people causing an insurgency and a Sunni/Shia military conflict. After a civil war in Iraq, the Allies eventually withdrew, the Arab Spring flourished, ISIS filled the vacuum, the Russians annexed Crimea (and very recently became the de facto protector of President Assad of Syria), and in other parts of the old Ottoman Empire from Tunis and Libya to Syria and Turkey there was yet another "land grab" by newly created alliances and rulers leading to World War III. Once again eroding support due to decades of a flawed strategy resulting in a "land grab", Bush W's unachievable operational goals, and poor tactics are creating a "perfect storm" mirroring the errors of the loosing sides in the first two World Wars.

Is it comforting to know that this Third Great War, like the others, will eventually end? Perhaps, though viewed more cynically, the cycle will unfortunately repeat, and there will be a Fourth Great War, a fifth, a sixth and so on, easily predictable because old men have always found a way to get young people to fight for them.

It is because he read Barbara Tuchman's book, *The Guns of August*, and learned from history's mistakes, that John F. Kennedy was able to (and credited his ability to) avoid triggering a Third Great War in 1962 over Cuba. And so it is with his words that is the Epilogue of America First? Which One?

J. Rambler Perkins
January 2017

PROLOGUE

In 1990 during the Presidency of George H.W. Bush then Secretary of Defense Dick Cheyney received a top secret report of the three most likely military threats to the United States. The third most likely was an incident with North Korea; the second most likely was that Saddam Hussein would invade Kuwait; and the most likely was a nuclear attack on the World Trade Center and Wall Street to incapacitate the American financial market. Several months later Saddam Hussein invaded Iraq.

The reason President Bush and Vice President Dick Cheyney testified before the 9/11 Commission in secret and not under oath or on the record was not to protect Bush, but to protect Cheyney.

ELECTION NIGHT

Upstairs in the White House residence President Baker and his wife, Evelyn, are seated on the couch surrounded by family, friends and young children running up and down the main foyer. An aide walks over to the President, "Sir, I just spoke with GOP headquarters and they said Ohio is still too close to call."

President Arthur Conrad Baker stares at the TV screen in disbelief, where he sees a hotel ballroom filled with people as the band plays. A banner above the podium reads "Four More Years Re-Elect Baker/Crane." A speaker comes to the microphone, "and so my friends, while the hour is late, the President still fights and so must we. We must get out there and fight for leadership and values, strength and conviction..."

At the back of the ballroom, the press, TV cameras, photographers, and reporters are updating the viewers at home, "once again on election night it seems that we are going to bed with that Florida slogan from the 2000 election, 'too close to call'."

President Baker changes the channel to an identical scene on TV with the band playing, the press corps broadcasting live from the back of the ballroom, and with another politician at the podium addressing a crowd holding signs that read "Time for Change Elect Hamilton/Clark". The TV reporters are all saying the same thing, "Here in Los Angeles at the Democratic headquarters for the Hamilton/Clark campaign, aides say that the Governor is conceding nothing and that they expect to declare victory as soon as all the ballots are counted in Ohio."

In a CNN studio veteran anchor Stanley Ropert is broadcasting. He is using a map of the United States with states colored in either red or blue. The state of Ohio is blank. "So here's where we stand as of 3am on the east coast. President Baker in red currently has 266 electoral votes, while the challenger, Democratic California Governor Conrad Hamilton in blue, has 252 electoral votes. The first candidate to receive 270 Electoral College votes wins. Therefore, Ohio with its twenty electoral votes will decide this election and once all precincts report in, we should have the result some time tomorrow morning."

At the White House reporter Rob Black updates, "With a difference of only 535 votes in Ohio separating the President and Governor Hamilton, the write-in ballots will determine who will be the next President of the United States."

Against the background of an Ohio high school cafeteria, a large number of people carefully evaluate each ballot, holding them up to the light and examining them with a magnifying glass. In the cafeteria a local reporter, "Just this morning the

Ohio Board of Elections began recounting every ballot in the state insuring that every vote was properly cast and recorded."

At the White House one month later Robert Black reports, "Day thirty of the recount brought several unexpected events. First, the Ohio Elections Board has thrown out over six hundred votes for the President placing victory in the hands of Governor Hamilton. Second, for the first time since election night, Oklahoma Governor Susan Crane spoke with reporters. As you may remember Governor Crane was asked by the GOP and President Baker to run in the Vice President's place after he stepped aside for – quote unquote - health reasons."

At the TV news studio Stanley Ropert interviews the Republican Nominee for Vice President, "Governor Crane is a hard line conservative and married to one of the GOP's largest contributors, oil tycoon Calvin Crane."

Governor Susan Crane was born November 24, 1962 the day Jack Ruby killed Lee Harvey Oswald. Her mother descends from one of the oldest families in America, who perpetuate the myth that their ancestors were on the Mayflower. She and her ailing mother are members of the Daughters of the American Revolution. Although her family was well known as Northern Republicans, she has since been anything but after attending Duke University where she met her husband Calvin. After graduation they married and returned to his home state of Oklahoma where they had twin sons Travis and Buddy. While Calvin rose through the corporate offices of Haliburton, Susan graduated from law school at the University of Oklahoma. She entered private practice but was easily seduced to run for public office. In her first election she became the Lt. Governor and years later found herself in the Governor's Mansion with a seventy-eight percent approval rating. When the incumbent Republican Vice President was dropped from the ticket she was added by President Baker.

"This is so scandalous. First we win and then the Democrats do everything, including committing election fraud, to get our votes thrown out. I think we're going to have to go back to the courts."

Stanley asks, "Isn't that exactly what you did in the 2000 election?"

Susan argues, "No, that's just left wing Hollywood liberal spin."

Outside the United States Supreme Court tens of thousands of people wave signs and cheer for their candidate. As the ruling is read, hundreds of reporters race out of the courthouse all hoping to be first with the headline. "Finally, just moments ago, after fifty-five days of recounting and going back and forth from the Ohio Supreme Court to the United States Supreme Court, the nine justices have decided in a five to four ruling that the current results of the election stand, which means that in an upset Democrat Governor Conrad Hamilton of California has defeated incumbent President Baker. On January twentieth, Governor Hamilton will be sworn in as the forty-fifth President of the United States."

One month later, somewhere in the Persian Gulf, with a new President sworn in as Commander-in-Chief, a US Navy helicopter is flying in low, off the coast heading across the desert and out over the ocean.

The chopper is filled with a platoon of forty US Navy SEALs, heavily armed and wearing night vision goggles. They are being led by 37 year-old Colonel Tanner, a tall thin man, standing directly right behind the pilot who tells him, "We're two minutes out."

Tanner turns to his lieutenant, "Two minutes."

The SEAL lieutenant yells to his men, "Two minutes. Get ready."

In Washington D.C. at the Pentagons' National Military Command Center, known as NMCC, the Operations Center is packed with computers and control panels operated by lieutenants and captains. A map of the area in the Persian Gulf is on the large screen on the wall at the front of the room. The helicopter is visible on the screen as it moves across the water.

Top generals and colonels monitor every move on the screens under the supervision of military hawk Army General Baxter and Navy Vice Admiral Fitzgerald who spent his career in command of several aircraft carriers. Forty year old Major O'Connor, the officer in charge of the NMCC, begins to sweat when Vice Chairman of the Joint Chiefs of Staff, General James (Jimmy) Hunter enters.

Hunter was born and raised in the Bayou. His grandfather was a member of the 82nd Airborne Division during World War II who parachuted into Normandy on D-Day and was later wounded during Operation Market Garden, which ended his military service with the rank of Captain and awarded both the Purple Heart and the Silver Star. After the war his family started a wholesale seafood business at which Hunter would work after school and during the summers. His father was never drafted into the Vietnam War and for years he was ashamed of not having served while many of his high school buddies never came home. The day after Hunter graduated from high school he enlisted in the Marines and maintained an excellent performance rating until being seriously wounded in the 1983 Beirut bombing of the Marine barracks. His recovery and rehabilitation took almost two years which he did in ROTC at LSU. He earned a Bachelor of Arts in Near Eastern Studies and a Master's and a Doctorate in Education. He achieved the rank of Major before being deployed to the Gulf War in 1990 during which he was promoted to Lt. Colonel. By 9/11 he was just in his second month as a Brigadier General and a decade later when American forces returned from Iraq he came home as a Lieutenant General. He was immediately nominated by President Obama and confirmed by the US Senate to the rank of Four Star General and became a Member of the Joint Chiefs of Staff to which he was eventually named its Vice Chairman. Married with two grown daughters, his life had been dedicated to the Marine Corps and he was revered as a tough warrior. He never enjoyed hunting and was quoted as saying, "I've shot enough in my life and have seen such carnage that what pleasure could I ever get to killing for enjoyment." He did, however, admit to eating meat, particularly enjoying a great Porterhouse after a day on the lake fishing.

One of O'Connor's men says, "Major, Colonel Tanner's chopper is two minutes out." Everyone in the Operations Center sees the chopper flying very low, speeding over the water and heading towards a super yacht. The chopper descends to the ocean two hundred meters from the yacht and hovers over the water.

Inside, Tanner gives his men the green light, "Blue team go – Red team go."

"Good luck," shouts the pilot as out of each side of the chopper the SEALS jump into the water and make their way toward the yacht. The pilot speaks into his radio, "This is Alpha Bird One – SEALS are in the water."

"Roger, the SEALs have been deployed," responds a radio operator from the aircraft carrier, USS Nimitz, which is in the Persian Gulf, escorted by several cruisers and destroyers.

At NMCC the door to the Operations Center opens. In walks a lieutenant with a good looking man dressed in a suit named Andrew (Guy) Beeks. He walks over to Vice Chairman Hunter who tells him, "You're late."

"Nice to see you again General – where are we?"

Major O'Connor updates him, "Colonel Tanner's team is preparing to board the yacht."

As the SEALs swim and surround the yacht, they see five terrorists guarding the main deck. Colonel Tanner issues orders to his two junior officers, "Sergeant, on my order you take those guys out. Lieutenant, you and your squad come with me."

With silencers on their weapons, the Sergeant's men kill the guards. Tanner and the Lieutenant's squad scale the side of the yacht and enter. In the main hall, a SEAL takes out two more terrorists on the second floor landing. In the main hall there are steps leading upstairs and downstairs. Following behind the Lieutenant's men, the Sergeants' squad enters the main hall. They split into two groups – half head off to secure the main floor before going downstairs, while the other SEALs proceed upstairs. Shots are heard and grenades explode as Colonel Tanner leads the Lieutenant's squad downstairs.

At the bottom of the steps they take out two more terrorists. The hallway is empty. "Clear," announces a SEAL.

There are three doors along this corridor – one on each side and one in front. They breach the two side doors with grenades. The door in front of them opens and two terrorists fire at them, hitting one of the SEALs. They fire back killing the two terrorists, "Clear."

The Sergeant's voice comes over Colonel Tanner's radio: "The main floor and second floor are secure."

The squad enters the center doors killing three more terrorists inside. The Lieutenant reports to Tanner, "All clear."

In the Operations Center at the NMCC everyone listens to the communications between the SEALs and the Nimitz while observing the monitors. The Nimitz radio operator reports, "The SEALs have secured the target. They are commencing their search of the ship now."

Hunter comments, "They better find those explosives. Otherwise the President, the Secretary, and the Chairman are going to make us all eat shit."

Aboard the yacht, the SEALs are completing their search of the room which was once the main cabin but is now piled high with an assortment of engineering equipment. Some of the containers bear the *Skull and Crossbones* poison symbol, but the SEALs quickly search through everything and eventually find what they came for – a container with the very recognizable *Ionizing Radiation* symbol on its side. The Lieutenant closely examines it and turns to Tanner, "Colonel, we're too late. The package is gone."

At NMCC, Beeks overhears the radio message. Even though clearly the youngest person in the Operations Center he does not hold back, "Well if the shit ain't there it's because it took you three days to move this team into the theatre."

Although he holds the top rank in the room, Vice Chairman Hunter is not offended by Beeks' words. Rather, he throws up his hands in frustration and turns to his subordinate, "General Baxter you want to explain to our military expert here how long it takes to move a SEAL team stationed in the mountains of Afghanistan, get them to an airport, fly them to 5th Fleet Command in Bahrain, land them on the Nimitz, brief them..."

"It would be my pleasure sir," Baxter replies just as over the radio Tanner's voice is heard.

"This is SEAL Team Commander."

"Go ahead colonel, this is the Nimitz."

"We're in the forward cabin and other than some bomb making equipment, there's nothing left here."

At NMCC, Major O'Connor announces, "Gentlemen, the satellite is coming into range right now." On the main screen on the wall a live video feed of Tanner becomes clearer, although the image is still green and grainy. His men are behind him examining the equipment.

As he points, Beeks instructs Major O'Connor, "Zoom in on that table. Are we recording?"

"Yes sir, as best we can."

"Cause I can't make out anything."

Major O'Connor responds, "As soon as the original video is back on the Nimitz we will receive a clean satellite transmission."

"Send it to my office as soon as it's in." Beeks then turns to Hunter and says, "I'm outta here. General, I suggest you secure the target until we confirm what's on that tape."

Hunter, "I agree."

"Good," Beeks continues, "Jimmy, I'll see you later at the White House." As he leaves, he acknowledges the rest of the top US military officers with a somewhat sarcastic salute, "Gentlemen."

A moment passes and General Baxter offers his opinion of Beeks, "What an asshole."

Vice Admiral Fitzgerald, "I agree."

Hunter disapproves, "Well that asshole has the ear of the President and is this nation's leading expert in nuclear warfare, proliferation, terrorism..."

Baxter, "He's still a punk."

Hunter explains, "He graduated number one from MIT with a doctorate in astrophysics and aeronautical engineering and he's fluent in five languages including Arabic."

Beeks grew up in Oahu, Hawaii as the only son of a rear admiral attached to the United States Pacific Fleet at Pearl Harbor. His mother died tragically when he was in grade school and as a way to distract himself from the loss, he became a lover of science fiction novels. Even in his teens while his friends would spend weekends in Honolulu he would stay on base and eventually developed a fascination for planes and ships and how they might one day exist like the ships and fighters he read about when he was younger. Simply, he was a genius and legendary for being the first person ever nominated to and accepted at Annapolis, West Point, and the Air Force Academy. He has never been married, and to counter his nerd brain and his top secret CIA position, he exploits his good looks as a player in the Washington D.C. nightclub scene.

"Rumor has it that he can also conduct one hell of a symphony." As Hunter finishes he instructs Major O'Connor, "Send me a copy of that tape along with Tanner's debriefing as soon as it comes in."

"Yes sir."

As Hunter leaves, Baxter orders, "Major, do it."

O'Connor speaks into his head set, "NMCC to the USS Nimitz."

"USS Nimitz, go ahead."

"USS Nimitz you have a green light on the SEAL deployment to secure the target."

"Roger, green light the SEALs." The room is dark with many computers and control panels as the Nimitz Radio operator confirms on her headset. Immediately, on the Nimitz flight deck, hundreds of SEALs, fully armed, run onto waiting Sea Knight choppers. As the SEALs board, the choppers take off into the dead of night to reinforce and secure the target.

STATE OF THE UNION

Several days later at the White House, an SUV pulls up to the side gate and is approached by a police officer. The one driver says, "I'm here to pick up the budgets."

"ID please."

The guard takes the ID and walks into the security booth. Another guard checks underneath the vehicle with a mirror and opens the back hatch. The first guard comes back to the car and returns the ID. "You know where to go?"

"I do." The SUV drives off toward the West Wing.

Inside the Oval Office members of the National Security Council gather to brief the newly sworn-in President Conrad Hamilton. He is surrounded by Vice-Chairman of the Joint Chiefs General Jimmy Hunter, the CIA's Guy Beeks, General Baxter, Vice Admiral Fitzgerald, FBI Agent Natalie Collins who is a year or two younger than Beeks and the only woman in the room, the Secretary of Defense, the CIA Director, the Chairman of the Joint Chiefs, the White House Chief of Staff, and additional military personnel and political advisors.

Beeks, "Sir the bottom line is we don't know what they were doing there. It could be a radioactive device - it could be some bio-chemical weapon. It could also be nothing. It could be the size of a truck or fit into my briefcase."

"Clearly we need more intelligence," offers the Chief of Staff.

The Defense Secretary, "I agree."

Beeks, "The only way to get what we really need is to send in a team on the ground."

Chairman of the Joint Chiefs asks, "How soon can we get a team from Langley to the Persian Gulf?"

CIA Director, "CIA can get a team out in two hours. What about the FBI?"

Collins, "I'll send someone from my counter-terrorism task force."

CIA Director asks Collins, "You're not going?"

Collins, "I don't work for CIA anymore – and certainly not in the Middle East. When you have terrorists in Hawaii call the FBI; then I'm your girl."

The door from the outer office opens and a secretary walks up to the President, "Excuse me sir, the Secretary of Transportation has arrived."

President Hamilton tells his national security team, "Let's go do it."

Chief of Staff, "We'll reconvene via video conference in forty-eight hours. Thank you everyone."

As everyone rises and exits, Hunter walks over to the President, "I'm sorry I won't be able to join you tonight."

"Don't be ridiculous, you have more important things to do."

"I'll be back on the job in two days."

The secretary hands the President a gift wrapped package which he gives to Hunter, "General, this is for your daughter from my wife and me and wish her congratulations on her wedding."

"Thank you, Mr. President."

As they exit the West Wing the CIA Director tells Beeks, "Guy, I want you to go to the Gulf and serve as point. In fact, prepare to leave tonight."

In the parking lot Beeks notices White House staffers loading boxes into the same SUV which had recently entered the White House complex. He replies, "I was supposed to go to the State of the Union tonight. I'm bringing a date."

"Well not anymore. I need you on that plane. You're the best man we have and we need to find out what the hell is going on there before a bomb goes off in a major American city. Guy, I'll make it up to you."

Beeks notices the SUV and overhears the two White House staffers loading it.

"What is all this shit?"

"I think it's the budgets for tonight; hell of a lot of wasted paper."

Beeks asks the CIA Director, "Why the hell are they doing that today?"

In the Oval Office the President rises from behind his desk as Transportation Secretary John Wilson is escorted in, "John, I know you really didn't want to do this, but someone has to stay behind."

"It's my honor Mr. President."

"And I didn't pick you because you're the only Republican in my Cabinet."

"I didn't think so sir."

"Feel free to watch the speech here in the Oval and order whatever you want for dinner."

"Anything else I should know?" asks Secretary Wilson as the First Lady enters the Oval Office.

He notices his wife, "I'll be a moment my dear," as he reaches out his hand to her and smiles. He continues, "John we could brief you on how to be a President but I'm sure it won't come to that – after all – you're fourteenth in the line of succession."

"Come on, you don't want to be late," says the First Lady as she helps her husband put on his coat.

Secretary Wilson, "Mrs. Hamilton, what a pleasure to see you again."

She responds, "I actually saw your wife the other day at a Red Cross event."

"Yes, she did mention it."

The President and his wife leave the Oval Office as Wilson sits on the couch and pulls out his cellphone. The President's secretary turns on CNN whose camera is positioned directly at the exterior of the US Capitol.

On the other side of Pennsylvania Avenue the SUV from the White House has parked at the Capitol building. One officer of the Capitol Police is barely paying attention as the same two drivers carry the boxes inside.

Ten miles east of Washington D.C. at Andrews Air Force, Beeks exits a Lincoln Town car, runs across the tarmac, and boards an Air Force Gulfstream. "Let's get out of here."

The President and his wife exit their limousine surrounded by Secret Service agents and enter the Capitol.

On a commercial 737 airplane Hunter is dressed in civilian clothes sitting in first class. He reads a novel as a flight attendant hands him a glass of champagne. He looks up and says, "Thank you." As his eyes move back to his book he glimpses on his small video screen the inside of the US Capitol as the State of the Union is about to begin.

The room is filled with Senators and Representatives. Mrs. Hamilton is in the balcony. In the front rows are the Supreme Court Justices in their traditional black robes, the highest ranking generals and admirals, and Cabinet members.

The doors in the back of the chamber open. The Crier walks through, stops, and shouts, "Here Ye, Here Ye, Mr. Speaker, the President of the United States." Everyone applauds as the President enters and begins shaking hands.

Across town FBI counter terrorism expert Natalie Collins opens the door to her apartment and drops her bag on the floor. She walks into her bedroom and turns on her TV set. She falls onto her bed with her clothes on. On the TV, the President is about to deliver the State of the Union address – making his way to the podium. She falls asleep. "And so my fellow Americans, I am pleased to announce tonight that the era of big government is over, and a period of productive government is beginning. Here tonight we are all united, facing a bright future and assuring prosperity and freedom for all..."

"I think this is the same speech as his Inauguration."

"This one's worse," responds Kelly, the CNN Producer, as laughter fills the control room. She is in charge of the broadcast and oversees a team of technicians, assistant directors and co-producers. The President appears on all the screens. The phone rings. She picks it up, "This is Kelly. Oh hi sweetie. Did you finish your homework? Mommy will be home by midnight... Ok goodnight. Put daddy on the phone. Hi...Hello. Hello?"

All the TV monitors have suddenly gone black and the Director asks, "What the hell? Did we just go black? Did we just lose power?"

Kelly moves the phone away from her head, "What happened?"

"We must have lost power."

She asks, "Are we still broadcasting?"

"No," responds one of the Assistant Directors.

The Director, "Are you sure?"

"And neither is anyone else," responds one of the co-producers as everyone looks up and sees that all the monitors indicate the other networks broadcasting the speech have also gone black.

The TV in the Oval Office is also not broadcasting anymore. Secretary Wilson changes the channel hoping that will help but all the channels are black and an announcement can be heard, "We are temporarily experiencing technical difficulties."

The phone rings again. A technician answers, "Hello." Then another ring and another - then every phone. Kelly looks around and her entire team is scrambling to figure out what's happening.

Somebody shouts, "The feed must have been cut."

"Well, fix it," responds the Director.

One of the co-producers hands Kelly a phone, "Kelly, it's Rob at the White House."

"Not now."

Screaming to get Kelly's attention, "He says there's been an explosion!"

The control room goes silent as everyone freezes in disbelief. Kelly, demands, "I want playback in three, two, one, playback."

The TV monitor rewinds for three seconds and then plays the President delivering the State of the Union, "This nation shall not give into Terro..."

The screen goes black.

The door bursts open and a half dozen secret service agents enter the Oval Office. They run directly to Wilson, "Sir, you must come with us immediately."

In the control room Kelly picks up the phone. "Rob, what's going on at the White House?" She tells her team, "Get a camera on him now." Rob is standing in the shot holding his cell phone with Kelly on the other end. Secret service agents and White House police officers are running around, some with barking dogs, as the White House press corps goes live one by one on their networks. Over Rob's shoulder past the front façade of the White House an orange glow illuminates the Washington D.C. sky line.

At the security gate house Rob sees chaos, as West Wing staffers, plain clothed and uniformed Secret Service agents have guns drawn and White House police officers watch the security monitors. Some are on the phone. A phone rings and an officer answers it, "White House security gate 4."

The officer turns around and hands the phone to a Secret Service agent. Other agents run out of the West Wing. Wilson is rushed through the hallway as the agents shout: "Let's go, let's go. Move it. Out of the way. Clear the hall." Everyone moves to the side while others are pushed out of the way and knocked to the ground.

Outside, a motorcade of black SUVs wait by the entrance flashing red and blue lights. Secret Service agents with guns drawn surround the vehicles. The West Wing entrance doors swing open as Wilson and the agents get him into the vehicle. The agents hop on the sides of the SUVs and they speed off. Other Secret Service SUVs race in and out of the grounds as a White House police officer approaches the press corps followed by Secret Service agents.

Rob, on the phone, "Kelly, all I know is – hold on."

The police officer instructs everyone, "We are evacuating the White House. Everyone needs to leave now. We are in a code red."

Rob asks Kelly, "Did you hear that?"

"Yup," Kelly has two phones up to her ears. "Get out of there but stay on the line."

In the CNN control room one of the technicians announces, "The AP is reporting an explosion at the Capitol building."

"Oh my God," the Director is in shock.

Kelly yells, "Someone find Stanley in Atlanta and get him in the chair now."

The Assistant Director picks up the phone, "Hi this is control B we need Stanley Ropert in the chair right now. There's been an explosion at the State of the Union."

As people run in and out of the control room Kelly asks the Assistant Director, "How long?"

"They said two minutes. He's in the bathroom. Someone went to get him."

Kelly tells her Director, "As soon as you have an aerial shot and Stanley, go live with the Breaking News logo." Still with two phones to her ears she orders the Assistant Director, "Call Euro Satellite now. We better be first in Europe with this one."

"Look," responds the Assistant Director. They both see that one of the monitors shows multiple F-15 Strike Eagles taking off from the runway at Andrews Airforce Base.

A thousand miles away in Oklahoma, Governor Susan Crane and her husband Calvin Crane watch TV. Their screen is black. Susan, "Change the channel," as Calvin flips through the channels but they are all black. Her phone rings. Susan picks it up, "Hello." The TV picture comes back on -

BREAKING NEWS and says, "We interrupt this program for a special report."

"Good evening. Stanley Ropert reporting from CNN headquarters in Atlanta. Approximately five minutes ago, a massive explosion occurred at the Capitol building during the President's State of the Union Address."

In the control room Kelly and her team watch Stanley on the TV monitor. The Assistant Director announces, "Rob is ready."

Stanley on TV, "The Associated Press is reporting that the Capitol is completely engulfed in flames. People have been seen running out with severe burns and in some cases actually on fire."

Kelly, speaking into Stanley's earpiece, "Go to Rob."

Stanley on TV, "Capitol police have evacuated the area. Now we are going live to White House chief correspondent Rob Black who is standing on Pennsylvania Avenue just outside the gates of the White House. Rob what can you tell us?"

Standing on Pennsylvania Avenue on TV, "Within the last ten minutes there has been what appears to be a major explosion at the U.S. Capitol. The building is completely on fire. As you can see from these aerial shots, the Capitol has been virtually – totally destroyed, but we don't yet know what caused the explosion. Of course since 9/11, everyone's initial reaction is that we are probably looking at an act of terrorism, but that is just peculation at this point. The White House staff has confirmed that the President and the Vice

President were both in the Capitol building at the time of the explosion."

CNN shows pictures of massive flames shooting out from where the Capitol building's giant dome once was. It has been completely destroyed. People can be seen fleeing the area as police, fire and EMS personnel help the victims in make-shift triage locations. Everyone around the country and throughout the world is glued to their TV screens – in every home and bar, in every major city thousands stand shocked looking at jumbotrons. The images appear on every airplane, each monitor in each seat and on every channel including on a 737 somewhere in the sky over Kentucky where Hunter has fallen asleep still holding his book. A flight attendant pokes him in the arm, "Mr. Hunter."

No response. She tries again, "Mr. Hunter."

"Yeah."

"The captain has asked me to give you this message."

While he's reading it an announcement is made from the flight deck, "Ladies and Gentlemen this is your captain speaking. I understand many of you have seen the reports on your video screens." Hunter and the flight attendant make their way to the flight deck as the captain continues, "This is obviously a national emergency and so Air Traffic Control has ordered a nationwide ground stop. We have been instructed to return to Dulles." Hunter knocks on the cockpit door.

The door opens and Beeks walks into the Gulfstream cockpit. The pilot breaks the news to him, "Mr. Beeks we've been ordered by the Pentagon to turn around. There's been an explosion at the U.S. Capitol building."

Beeks, "What?"

"You can turn on the TV in the cabin."

Beeks walks back into the cabin. He turns on CNN and sees Rob continuing his report from Pennsylvania Avenue, "We can also confirm at this time that almost every member of Congress and all nine members of the Supreme Court were in the building at the time of the explosion."

Natalie Collins is asleep on a couch. Her beeper goes off. Her phone rings. Her cell phone rings. There is a knock at the door – banging on the door. She eventually wakes up and picks up her cell phone. She yells to the door, "Hold on." She answers her phone, "Hello." With more banging at the door, she speaks into the phone, "Hold on," and then yells towards the door, "One second!" Wearing her clothes she wore the day before, she walks to the door looking at her beeper. She looks at the clock. It reads "9:50". "Who is it?"

Collins grew up in Fargo, North Dakota in a family of practicing Lutherans who emigrated from Scandinavia. Although socially conservative, she accepted a full academic scholarship to Smith College, a prestigious liberal leaning all women's university in the Massachusetts Berkshire Mountains. She went on to earn a Doctorate in International Relations from George Washington University and was working in the State Department when she was recruited into a CIA training program. As threats of ISIS sympathizers materialized in the United States she was transferred to FBI

Headquarters. She leads a very private life, never wears anything but pantsuits and was briefly engaged to a lawyer whom she left after discovering that he was cheating on her.

At Dulles airport the 737 has pulls up to a gate, and the plane door opens from which Hunter exits. Inside the terminal, several military personnel calmly stand just outside the jet-way waiting for Hunter. The gate area is jammed-packed with nervous, scarred, and crying passengers. When Hunter approaches them they salute, "General, this way sir." They exit the terminal by walking down some steps and onto the tarmac and enter an SUV in which small screens broadcast the news coverage.

On CNN Stanley looks visibly shaken. He clears his throat and removes his glasses, "With extreme sorrow, we must inform our viewers that the White House and the Secret Service have confirmed that both President Hamilton and Vice President Clark have been killed this evening." In the Gulfstream, Beeks watches as the plane lands at Andrews Air Force Base. Stanley continues, "We can also report that the leadership of the House and the Senate are among those who have lost their lives tonight. Let us offer our prayers to their families and all Americans." He pauses, "All right let's go back to Rob Black at the White House."

It's not long before Hunter enters the NMCC Operations Center at the Pentagon. Major O'Connor is in charge. The room is bustling with military officers running all about and shouting into the phones and at each other.

O'Connor's greeting, "General Hunter."

"What's the status?"

"All airspace over Washington has been cleared. General Baxter scrambled the F-15's out of Andrews. They're patrolling over DC and he is holding on the line from NORAD."

Hunter asks, "Where are the Chairman and the Secretary of Defense?"

O'Connor answers, "The Chairman was killed along with the entire Cabinet."

"Who's in charge?"

"Secretary Wilson was evacuated from the White House and is on route to Evac Station C at Camp David."

"No, who's in charge of military command?"

"You are sir."

General Baxter appears on the monitor on the wall.

Hunter acknowledges him, "General Baxter, take us to DEFCON 2 and put the Nimitz on ready alert."

Baxter replies, "Yes Sir."

"Also let's land all aircraft, commercial and private, in the U.S. until we rule out a coordinated plane attack."

"It's already done."

At Camp David President Wilson, his wife, and a judge dressed in a black robe stand together as Wilson takes the oath of office. White House staff members and secret service agents with guns drawn witness the oath as a White House photographer takes pictures.

"...and will to the best of my ability preserve, protect and defend the Constitution of the United States."

The Judge, "Congratulations, Mr. President." The new first lady hugs her husband with tears running down her cheeks.

Within minutes of taking the oath of office, President Wilson is on video conference from the Camp David Situation Room surrounded by aides and military officers. The only one who stands out is carrying the "football," the briefcase containing the nuclear codes and protocols . At the NMCC Operations Center Major O'Connor tells Hunter, "President Wilson is on video conference from Camp David."

Hunter sees the new Commander-in-Chief, "Mr. President."

"General Hunter, I'm appointing you acting Chairman of the Joint Chiefs."

"Proud to serve, Sir - particularly at this tragic time."

President Wilson's first order, "Immediately secure our borders, close all airports and ports, organize a task force to investigate this, and you and your team be at the White House tomorrow morning – 6am."

"Sir, you don't want to meet now?"

"General, I have a nation to comfort and a government to form tonight."

Beeks and Collins walk in together as President Wilson reiterates, "You're in charge. Assemble your team. Keep us updated and we'll talk in the morning."

On the main screen at the Operations Center everyone goes silent as CNN shows footage of President Wilson being sworn in. Narrating the coverage, Stanley announces, "This is just coming in. In this footage just released by the White House Communications Office, you can see former Secretary of Transportation John Wilson being sworn in as the forty-fifth President of the United States."

The broadcast continues with Stanley interviewing Susan Crane. "Governor Crane, thanks for joining us from Oklahoma at this difficult time. Now that President Wilson has been sworn in, what's the next step?"

"Thank you Stanley. First, I'd like to extend my condolences to the families of those who perished in this terrible event."

"I'm sure everyone around the world expresses the same thoughts and prayers."

Governor Crane continues, "With respect to the government, both the Democrat Governors' Caucus and the Republican Governors' Caucus will be convening via teleconference overnight to appoint an interim House and Senate. I'm sure the President will nominate cabinet positions and Supreme Court jurists for Senate confirmation within the next several days."

Stanley asks, "What about figuring out who's responsible? How will we proceed with an investigation to determine who's behind this attack?"

"I'm sure the new President will meet with his generals and all assets of the United States will be used to hunt down and kill those responsible."

"To kill them?"

"We must redouble our efforts in fighting groups like ISIS, Boko Haram, and Al Qaeda. We must wipe radical Islamic fighters off the face of the earth."

"Governor, I just hope that whoever is responsible for this -- we take action against them and not get into another sink hole like Iraq."

"What does that mean?"

"The U.S. invaded Iraq, even though it was Al Qaeda who attacked us on 9/11, and then we couldn't get out of there. And when we finally did, the Middle East was set ablaze."

"Again, I will say we must defeat radical Islam."

THE NEXT DAY

Hailing from the State of Texas, John Wilson lived the life of a traditional Republican politician. The son of a high school teacher and a librarian he graduated from the University of Texas and attended the Yale Law School where he made Law Review. After returning to Texas, he clerked for the United States Court of Appeals for the Fifth Circuit. He served as a federal prosecutor with one of the highest conviction rates and became well known for prosecuting Timothy McVeigh in 1995. He was elected Texas Attorney General and eight years later he was elected Governor. Although greatly admired for his moral values and religious lifestyle within the national Republican Party, he failed to win his party's nomination in their last contested presidential primary.

The following morning at the White House, the sun is shining brightly, without a cloud in the sky. Pennsylvania Avenue is blocked off by the police and Secret Service. Four black SUVs drive past the White House, pass through a security gate, and stop in front of the West Wing. Hunter, Vice Admiral Fitzgerald, Beeks, Collins, and several other military officers exit the SUVs and proceed to their meeting in the Oval Office.

While they walk, Beeks argues with Collins, "The Middle East desk at Langley is convinced we're talking about Islamic fundamentalists. Why do you insist it's not?"

She responds, "It's like any other crime. Means – opportunity – motive. What's the motive?

"The motive is to get us out of the Middle East so they can create a caliphate."

"And you do that by taking out the US government and putting a Republican in the White House?"

"Be realistic. If they didn't do it, then who the hell did?"

"Listen, on 9/11 we lost three thousand Americans and in retaliation invaded two countries. If they want us out of the Middle East to create a caliphate, they don't do something that even they know will lead to an all-out war in the Arab World. They're crazy, not stupid. It doesn't make any sense."

Just outside the Oval Office, the Secret Service maintains the highest level of vigilance as they stand at their posts. As they enter, Beeks whispers to Collins, "If you tell the President it wasn't Islamic terrorists, he's going to think you're crazy."

As day breaks in Oklahoma, Susan is speaking on the phone. Calvin is also on the phone but sitting at a desk. A black woman dressed in an outdated black and white maid's uniform enters the room and serves coffee.

Susan is in a political mindset, "Well I assume The President will appoint a cabinet and jurists that are consistent with our conservative Republican philosophy."

Calvin whispers to her, "You should be the V.P."

In the Oval Office, the President, Hunter, Vice Admiral Fitzgerald, Beeks, Collins, some military officers and White House staffers are meeting.

Beeks suggests, "Well sir, regarding method, we're sure it was a bomb and not a missile or a plane. In terms of who did this, at this point we have three possibilities. I think we were attacked by terrorists, Natalie believes..."

"I can speak for myself. I believe the odds of foreign terrorists pulling off something like this is one in a million. I think we're more likely looking at some sort of domestic plot."

The President asks, "What's the third possibility?"

Collins answers him, "It was an attack to change the government, not to destroy it -- essentially a coup d'état."

Hunter asks, "What about a foreign government?"

Beeks answers, "State doesn't believe that's what we're looking at. But we'll know more once Natalie and I get down to the Capitol and meet with FBI forensics."

The disagreement continues in the hall just outside the Oval Office with Hunter telling Beeks and Collins, "If this was a coup, you two will have to look at everybody."

Beeks, "At least those that are still alive."

Hunter is concerned, "Well, find out quickly before we end up at war with the wrong people. If the President believes

Islamic fundamentalists are behind this, he'll bomb the shit out of the Middle East. Most important, find out if it's over, or if more attacks are coming."

The investigation begins at the FBI forensics lab which looks like all the forensics labs on TV put together. Beeks and Collins are being briefed by the Chief forensics scientist, a very senior man both in years at the agency and in life. The Chief asks, "Do you want to hear about the bomb?"

"Save it. It exploded and everyone died." Beeks is still agitated from listening to Collins' ridiculous theories and annoyed with Hunter for entertaining them.

"Andrew," Collins realizes that the Chief was just insulted. "Sorry Chief, we haven't slept in days."

The Chief reports, "Your explosive was the equivalent of two five thousand pound bunker busters. It could have sunk an aircraft carrier. The good news is that it wasn't released from a plane. It was already in the Capitol when was it detonated. We know this because when a bunker buster is stationary when it detonates, it blows up and out far more that if you were to fire it from a plane or a ship. Plus, any plane able to carry such weapons would have been picked up on radar."

Collins asks, "So it was definitely in the building before it exploded?"

Beeks adds, "How the hell did it get there?"

After being insulted the Chief is frustrated with Beeks, "that's your job to figure out." He returns to his work station that is covered with his lunch and turns on CNN.

Rob White is reporting from the White House lawn over historical footage. "Good evening. In the latest report from the White House, we have learned that President Wilson has nominated four conservative jurists and five others who are considered moderate to liberal. President Wilson said that he wanted to maintain the same balance on the court that existed before the attack on the Capitol. The White House also said today that the Vice Presidential nominee will be announced tomorrow and of course will require confirmation by the Senate. To put this into historical perspective, the last time something like this happened was in 1973, when Speaker of the House Gerald Ford was appointed VP by then President Richard Nixon, following Vice President Spiro Agnew's resignation after he pleaded no contest to tax evasion and money laundering. As you may remember, Ford became President in 1974 after Nixon resigned due to the Watergate scandal."

In Oklahoma, Susan and Calvin Crane are also watching CNN. Rob continues, "Some of our sources are saying that as part of the healing process for the nation, the President will probably nominate a Democrat, perhaps a current governor or even a former Secretary of State."

Calvin suggests, "Susan, you need to get on a plane and meet with Wilson tomorrow. You should be appointed. You've earned it."

"He'll never do it."

"Well, you can be frank with him. Tell him he either appoints you or he will have a very short term. We'll put our energies someplace else."

In the Oval Office twenty-four hours later, the President and Susan sit alone opposite each other. Susan tries to make her case, "I understand that for the sake of the country, you want to maintain the status quo. However, as a Republican I'm sure you would agree that a strong Republican executive branch is also in our nation's best interest."

"I appreciate your thoughts. However, I have decided to go with the Democratic governor from Florida."

"You're going with Martinez? He's as liberal as they come. He's a Mexican. He would make every illegal a citizen tomorrow."

"I understand you are disappointed. Maybe you should think about an ambassadorship or even a cabinet post, once things settle down."

"Don't be a fool. If you don't make me Vice President, you know I can destroy you."

The President stands up, smiles and extends his hand. Susan stands, but doesn't shake his hand.

"Good day Susan. I think you're looking to bite off more than you can chew. Don't go searching for trouble. Right now this nation needs to stand together."

Susan storms out.

A few blocks from 1600 Pennsylvania Avenue at FBI Headquarters Collins and Beeks are reviewing their evidence.

Beeks ponders to himself, "So how did the bomb get into the Capital?"

"Someone on the inside you think?"

"Must be."

She suggests, "So let's assume the explosives were in the containers on that SUV you saw since Capitol security records indicate that the only truck allowed access to the building that evening was the truck carrying the budgets."

He agrees, "That's how they must have done it. Did you put out an APB on that truck?"

"Chances are it is long gone, but if it's still here, we'll find it."

Beeks hopes, "Maybe we'll get lucky. Don't forget the first group to bomb the World Trade Center wanted a refund on the deposit for the truck they used to detonate the bomb and that's how we caught them."

An FBI agent walks in and informs them, "State Police got a tip from a clerk at a motel. We think we've got the truck and we have the driver in custody."

In an FBI interrogation room the prisoner is sitting in a chair in the middle of the room and there is no other furniture. Beeks and Collins walk in.

In Arabic, Beeks begins, "So you're the one that is going to be charged with the murder of the President of the United States."

The prisoner looks down.

Beeks continues in Arabic, "If you think you are a hero for your Muslim brothers you are kidding yourself. No one knows you exist, and you will be held by our government indefinitely. And while you are waiting we will destroy your family."

The prisoner answers him in English, "You don't know what you're talking about."

Collins asks, "What do you mean?"

He says nothing.

Beeks, "So you do speak English."

The prisoner, "I say nothing."

Beeks goes back to Arabic, "I'll be direct, you either answer us truthfully or I will remove a piece of your body. You know the rumors about American soldiers torturing Muslims?"

Collins clears her throat at Beeks. Beeks is surprised that she understands Arabic. The prisoner looks scared.

Beeks continues, "They're all true. So, let's start with a simple question. How did you get access to the Capitol and who is your contact in the White House?"

The prisoner says nothing.

As Beeks opens the door, two CIA agents walk in with two military officers and he orders them, "Strip him."

As they do Beeks asks Collins, "So what do you think?"

"Food denial and sleep deprivation?"

He responds, "We don't have time."

She concurs, "I agree. What about truth serum?"

"The Israelis don't find it very effective and it takes at least a week."

She offers a suggestion, "I hate to say it, but since we have ongoing presidential authority, go for it. I'd chop off a finger first, since he'll probably think you're bluffing, and after that tell him you'll chop off his jewels."

Beeks brags, "It won't be my first circumcision."

Collins doesn't want to be there when he does it, "Just hurry it up.   I'm going for coffee."   She exits the interrogation room and closes the door.

While Beeks begins his interrogation in D.C., in Oklahoma Susan and Calvin Crane are having dinner in their dining room.   "Calvin, when I threatened him he threatened me back."

"So let's go to the next level."

Susan asks, "What do you mean?"

"Convene the Republican Governors' Caucus and secede. I'll call my guys and we'll guarantee the support of the governors.   With their support you'll control half the US National Guard."

She's concerned, "We'll have nothing more than a militia."

Calvin expresses his wisdom, "We'll have power and then we'll cut a deal.   It's not like there's any court we can go to for a remedy.   Besides, moderates in the Blue States will align with us.

Susan prays, "Let's hope so."

While the politicians politic, the investigators investigate. At FBI headquarters, Collins is asleep at her desk when Beeks walks in holding coffee.   The clock reads 6am; CNN is on.   He hands her the coffee, "I stopped at Starbucks."

She asks, "How late were you up with him?"

"It took less than an hour."

"Is he dead? Don't tell me that. I'm with the FBI now – I don't want to know. Just tell me, did you get what we needed?"

Beeks answers, "He was hired by a law firm downtown and yes he is alive – and yes he has all his fingers as well as his jewels."

On CNN in Collins' office, Stanley Ropert is in the anchor chair with BREAKING NEWS. "We go live right now to Chief White House correspondent, Rob Black."

"Thank you Stanley. It appears the Constitution and our greater American union may be in grave jeopardy this morning. The Associated Press is reporting that Oklahoma Governor and former Vice Presidential candidate Susan Crane has announced the call-up of the Oklahoma Nation Guard. Governors of several states have followed suit. As of now they include Kansas, Alabama, Mississippi, Georgia, and Texas."

Upon hearing this Beeks looks at Collins, "The country is collapsing. We've got to track down that law firm."

Collins jumps up, "Let's go."

In Oklahoma at the Crane Ranch, Calvin sits in his worn out leather chair. He's smoking a cigar and holding a scotch. There are two other gentlemen with him. One is noted Washington D.C. attorney Skip Garrison, and the other is one of the wealthiest oil drillers and bankers in America, the obese and infamous Howard Mellon from Pittsburgh.

Calvin says, "I'm sending my boy, Buddy, to San Diego. General Baxter is moving to within one hundred miles of the naval port. He believes he can seize the ships within twenty-four hours."

Skip is confidant, "General Baxter will be able to see this through. He's a patriot."

Calvin asks, "How far do you want to take this?"

Mellon answers, "Well the President and the Senate will either agree to shared power or we'll control all the Red States."

Skip is confidant, "Howard, don't worry. We've been doing this since the 1950s. Do you really think that elections determine our leaders? No, we do. We decide who gets the money. We've been orchestrating elections forever and the couple of hundred votes the Democrats stole in Ohio still doesn't make this a democracy. You're still running things."

Mellon, "Just make sure we don't have another Watergate. I'm not going through what my father dealt with."

Skip walks over to Mellon and looks him in the face, "Your father was my father's client. My name's on the firm – we'll take care of everything.

Skip and Mellon shake hands before Skip leaves the room. Once he's gone, Calvin tells Mellon, "Don't worry, there's no Howard Hunt Jr. running our operation."

In Washington D.C. at the law firm of GARRISON, ROPES, & WELSH LLP, Collins and Beeks approach the reception desk along with a team of federal agents.

"Can I help you?" asks the receptionist.

"I'm Natalie Collins with the FBI and we'd like to see Skip Garrison."

"He's not in."

Collins presents a document, "This is our search warrant. Please call a senior accounting officer. We want to speak with them as well."

At the White House, President Wilson has called Hunter into the Oval Office for an emergency meeting. The President breaks the bad news, "Baxter has left NORAD. He's now working for Susan Crane."

Hunter informs the President, "We've secured all of our ballistic nuclear missiles. Baxter is two days away from taking the San Diego naval port. We need to move the fleet into the Pacific, now."

"Hunter get out there immediately. Oversee it and prepare for a counter attack."

At the law firm of GARRISON, ROPES, & WELSH LLP Collins, Beeks, and the federal agents are finally making progress after reviewing every file in Skip Garrison's office. Several agents interview the secretaries while others examine computers. One announces, "We found something."

Collins and Beeks approach the agent reviewing the computer and he shows them a file, "Here it is - a purchase order for your truck."

Collins asks the secretary, "Where is Skip Garrison?"

"He's in the Midwest."

Beeks asks the secretary, "Can you pull up a list of his contacts?"

"That would fall under attorney client privilege."

Collins interjects, "Thanks to the Patriot Act there is no privilege. Besides we're not interested in his clients, we're investigating him for murder and treason."

Beeks, "Natalie, look at this."

Beeks, Collins and the agent are looking at the computer. On the screen, a list of Garrison's contacts appears. They notice that Clarence Wilson is on the list. Beeks thinks out loud, "What's the connection between Garrison and Wilson?"

Collins asks the secretary, "How well does Mr. Garrison know President Wilson?"

"I believe they went to Yale together."

At the San Diego Air Base at Miramar, Hunter and other military officers exit a Learjet and approach the waiting SUVs. Admiral Fitzgerald greets Hunter.

Hunter quickly asks for a status report.

"We've moved the Ronald Reagan, the Stennis, and the brand new CVN-77 to about 150 miles off the coasts of San Diego and Los Angeles. Their accompanying battle groups are being deployed now."

"What about aircraft?"

"Two squadrons, approximately one hundred fighter jets, mainly from bases in Nevada and the California desert, have defected to the other side. All other aircraft have been redeployed to Blue States, primarily in the northeast and the northwest. We also have aircraft patrolling above all major US cities."

Hunter asks, "Where's Baxter?"

Fitzgerald continues, "He's got Governor Crane's troops fifteen miles from the port. He has a division of ten thousand soldiers, about 200 tanks, and a similar number of armored and transport vehicles all waiting for the go order. No movement yet though."

Not far off in the California desert, Calvin and Susan's son, Buddy Crane, exits one of the landing helicopters and is greeted by General Baxter.

He asks Baxter, "When are you deploying?"

Our forward deployed troops are two miles to the east of San Diego. They should enter the city within the hour."

While an American Civil War appears unavoidable on the west coast, in Washington D.C. late into the night Collins and Beeks examine their case files in Collins' FBI office.

Beeks, "So our theory now is that this Garrison lawyer hired the terrorists."

Collins, "Yeah, but for who? Who was he working for and what was his motive?"

He suggests, "Let's assume that Garrison and Wilson were in on this together. Was their motive to take over the office of the President of the United States?"

"If you're right, how could Wilson have known that he was to be the cabinet secretary asked to stay behind during the State of the Union?"

"And how could we ever prove it?"

Collins expresses concern, "If we're right and the White House finds out what we're on to, you know they'll kill us."

"How would they ever find out?"

"What about Hunter? We'll need to tell him what we're thinking."

Beeks states, "He can be trusted."

"Would you risk your life on it?"

"I would."

Collins suggests, "There is another possibility we should consider. Perhaps Wilson was framed."

RED, WHITE, & BLUE

In San Diego, the sun sets over the Pacific Ocean. On the streets, Baxter's forces enter the downtown area and advance toward the port. M2A3 Bradleys, M1 Abrams tanks, and Humvees slowly drive through the city with soldiers following behind before splitting off down the side streets advancing on the port.

In the CNN studio, Stanley Ropert anchors, "We interrupt this program for breaking news out of San Diego." News helicopters cover the attack like it was an LA police chase. On the empty streets of San Diego, police officers fire at Baxter's soldiers. His tanks return fire, destroying most of the police cars. Stanley continues, "As you can see from these pictures, military forces backing the so-called "Red State" break-away government led by Governor Susan Crane have entered the downtown area of San Diego. Tanks are rolling through the city as thousands of soldiers advance toward the naval port. White House correspondent Rob White is joining us live, from San Diego. Rob, what can you report?"

The San Diego border with Mexico is closed. Cars are backed up for miles. Baxter's men advance under fire as the soldiers under Hunter's command defend their positions. Rob reports, "Thanks Stanley. It appears that soldiers loyal to the break-away Red State government, which now calls itself the Confederated States, have taken military control of downtown San Diego. This exclusive aerial footage shows that for the first time in one hundred and fifty years, two groups of American soldiers are battling each other."

The Confederated States soldiers have captured the port but failed to secure any ships because Hunter was able to reposition the Union navy miles out to sea. The battle is over – General Baxter and Governor Crane's Confederated Army have won the first battle.

On an Air Force Learjet, Hunter is speaking on the phone while Fitzgerald, sitting across from him, is also on the phone. Fitzgerald hangs up and tells Hunter the bad news, "We lost San Diego."

Hunter responds, "Order them to retreat to Orange County and protect the nuclear reactor at San Onofre."

An aide approaches them, "NMCC on line three."

Hunter picks up the phone and hears a report, "Chairman Hunter, General Baxter has moved an armored infantry division to within one hundred miles of Las Vegas. It's on TV right now."

Hunter tells his aide, "Turn on the TV." The aide does.

The broadcast shows everyone in the Las Vegas casinos watching the news on every TV channel. On CNN Rob reports, "What is now being called the Confederate Army is, according to the Associated Press, advancing towards Las Vegas and could enter the city sometime tonight." As soon as the gamblers hear his words, everyone in the casinos runs for the exits in a mad rush trampling over each other.

In the Nevada desert just outside Las Vegas, General Baxter exits his Humvee. A Colonel approaches him, "We'll rest here for two hours and take the city in the morning."

"Colonel, just make sure the airport is closed."

The Colonel replies, "Planes are taking off as quickly as the airlines can turn them around. I think we're better off letting people evacuate. People are fleeing north and east of the city in cars. Let's let them leave. Holding them hostage will just complicate matters."

"I don't care about hostages."

A soldier approaches him, "Phone call for you, General."

"Baxter here."

"General, it's Calvin. I'm sitting here with the guys. We want to know how long before we can take Washington DC."

Baxter responds, "The day after tomorrow."

The next morning, Collins is sitting in her FBI office staring at her computer when Beeks walks in.

She says. "Guess what I found on Yale's website?"

He offers her, "Coffee?"

"Yeah. Thanks."

He looks at her computer, "So what did you find?"

"Guess who else went to Yale with Garrison?"

Jokingly, "Tom Brady?"

"Who? How about Calvin Crane."

"Susan Crane's husband?"

Collins explains, "Her husband is also a steel and oil tycoon. All three were in the same fraternity."

"We need to brief Hunter."

As the sun rises over the western desert in San Diego the next morning, Confederate soldiers enter a government Detention Center for illegal aliens. Although the guards draw their guns, they are easily overtaken by the soldiers.

A Confederate major steps forward and approaches the Detention Center's administrator, "This facility is now under the control of the Confederate Army. Effective immediately, you are all prisoners. This building is completely surrounded. If you surrender, your men's lives will be saved."

The administrator responds, "We don't work for the military, and you are not part of the American army. You are rebels and you are all under arrest."

"I think not." The Major pulls out his pistol and shoots the administrator in the head. All of the Major's men draw their guns. "Anybody else?" threatens the Major.

The detention guards drop their guns.

The Major, "All right men gather the illegals. They're all going back to Mexico."

At the White House in the Oval Office, President Wilson admits to Hunter, "I never thought it would come to this."

Hunter responds, "Sir, we should consider that we could face an attack on the east coast within a few days."

"What makes you say that?"

"Because that's what I would do. We need to prepare a defense of D.C. and the White House. If they capture this building it's a great victory for them, even if you're able to escape. Susan Crane will deliver a victory speech from the East Room, announcing to the world that you are no longer the President"

"What about our nuclear weapons?"

Hunter assures him, "Everything has been secured."

"And the investigation, do we have any leads?"

Hunter responds, "I'm meeting with Beeks and Collins later today."

The President tells Hunter, "Just keep me informed."

A CNN broadcast shows Confederate soldiers escorting Mexican Americans across the border back into Mexico. Stanley continues, "As this struggle moves into its second week, it appears that Confederate soldiers have taken control of all major cities in the southwest with the exception of Los Angeles. We have learned that Los Angeles is being protected by the California National Guard and two armored Marine divisions."

"With their military success, the Confederate government has enacted a series of laws imposing social changes in keeping with their political views." On the screen, Planned Parenthood facilities are shown surrounded by Confederate soldiers and being closed. "In a statement issued by Governor Crane's office earlier today, the Confederacy has placed a ban on abortion, repealed federal taxes for anyone making over one million dollars a year, and issued an

Executive Order giving illegal aliens two weeks to leave the U.S. or face 'aggressive state action' -- whatever that means. Also, all US attorneys in states under confederated control have been replaced by Governor Crane's appointees."

Watching TV in the Crane living room report their success, Calvin Crane, Andrew Mellon, and Skip Garrison are celebrating with drinks. Susan walks in, "What's up gentlemen?"

Her husband responds, "General Baxter informed us that we are ready to begin the advance on Washington tomorrow."

She suggests, "I think we should wait. They're weak. We can probably negotiate a good deal and get what we want."

Mellon doesn't want to hear any of this, "I, and before me my father, have been running the Republican Party for more than a century. We built this country, financed two world wars and defeated the Soviets. We've eliminated and impeached presidents, framed senators and removed judges, and we only got caught once thanks to Nixon. If I say we go tomorrow, we go tomorrow. There's nothing to negotiate. When we're in the White House, they'll negotiate with us."

Calvin looks at Susan for her reaction as she replies, "I don't really know what you're talking about but I'll go along...for now."

Mellon instructs Susan, "If you want to meet with Wilson then do it, but use our leverage. He either makes you number two or he resigns. I really don't care which. He won't run again anyway, so if he wants to be President for a couple years, fine, as long as he knows we call the shots."

In Collins' office at FBI Headquarters, Hunter, Collins, and Beeks discuss the investigation. Collins offers, "We're pretty sure this was not Islamic terrorists."

Hunter asks, "What leads you to believe that?"

Collins answers, "Well sir, we have the truck driver who delivered the bomb to the Capitol in custody, and the information he provided eventually led us to a DC lawyer named Garrison, Skip Garrison."

Hunter, "I know him. He's with Ropes and something. Walsh or Welsh."

She clarifies, "Welsh, sir."

Beeks says, "Jimmy, the bottom line is that while the explosive devices probably came from overseas, the conspiracy was domestic."

Collins continues, "Sir, I was in the Persian Gulf and I saw the bomb materials there. Those specific parts are all needed to cause such extensive damage using the type of explosives FBI forensics say were detonated at the Capital. The only problem is that while the bomb components could easily get through customs, how the hell did it get through security at the Capital?"

Hunter, "Who are your suspects?"

Beeks answers, "Well, Garrison and the President are old friends from their college days."

"What are you suggesting?"

Collins, "He's not the only one who is connected to Garrison. Calvin Crane also knew him well."

Hunter asks, "So now what?

Collins responds nodding to Beeks, "We will continue investigating."

As he leaves Collins' office Hunter advises, "Make it quick because the country is on the brink of war."

Collins and Beeks are left alone in the office.

Collins, "Hunter's right you know."

"About what?"

"About everything," she explains. "I mean either President Wilson was behind it, or he knew about it, or those responsible made sure that Wilson wasn't going to be at the State of the Union speech." Pondering, "Or maybe he's being framed – but by who, and for what reason?"

"If he wasn't a part of the conspiracy then why did they select him?"

She suggests, "Because they felt they could influence him because he's a Republican, or they already controlled him. For all we know, they have some pictures of him with a teenage girl or even juicier, maybe he 'trumped' several of them at once."

"And in this grand conspiracy of yours who is 'they'?"

The next day on the radio, "Good morning New York. It's 6am and time for your world headlines. The stock market has stabilized. Yesterday the DOW closed down only two percent, the smallest decline since the State of the Union tragedy."

In Washington DC it is also a beautiful morning. Grounds crews are working at the White House as construction workers are clearing out debris from the Capitol. In the distance across the Potomac River, a plane lands at Reagan Airport. It pulls into a hanger. Susan Crane and Skip Garrison exit the plane surrounded by body guards and aides. The two enter a limo and the motorcade leaves.

The radio report continues, "The White House has announced that a meeting between President Wilson and Governor Crane will take place this morning to consider how best to resolve this national tragedy."

At a coffee shop in Washington DC, Beeks and Collins enjoy a morning cup of java. Collins' phone rings, "Hello. Really? All right, secure him there." She asks Beeks, "Guess who just showed up at his Office?

"Who?"

"Garrison. They've placed him under guard and await further instructions."

At the White House, Susan Crane enters the Oval Office and shakes President Wilson's hand. "Good morning John. Good of you to see me on such short notice."

"Hello Susan. Thanks for coming. We've certainly gotten ourselves into one big mess."

They both sit down. Crane bodyguard and two Secret Service agents are the only other people in the room.

The President continues, "I'll get right to the point. The Federal government will grant your rebels immunity so long as your army ceases all military actions. For the sake of the country and the world, this conflict needs to end now."

"Appoint me Vice President, maintain the Executive Orders we've introduced, and you have a deal."

The President is about to say something, but he thinks for a moment. He then nods his head in the affirmative. Susan interjects, "You also must agree not to run in four years."

He asks, "Do I have a choice?"

She responds, "Even if you run and win, you will never serve a second term, and you know it. You didn't play ball when you should have. It's out of my hands now and you know whose hands it's in."

At his law firm, Skip Garrison is sitting on the couch in his office with a guard stationed outside his door. Collins knocks. As Beeks and Collins enter, she asks, "Do you want to take the lead here or do you want me to handle this?"

Beeks responds, "I've got it." Collins smiles as he begins, "Mr. Garrison, we've been dying to talk to you."

Skip asks, "Who are you? What can I do for you?"

"This is Natalie Collins with the FBI and I'm..."

Collins interrupts him, "We're investigating the Capitol bombing and your name keeps coming up."

"I don't know how. I wasn't even in Washington..."

Beeks points at him, "You were the middle man between Calvin Crane and the people responsible for the bombing of the Capitol and killing and maiming hundreds of people. Not to mention that it was you who got that SUV into the Capitol complex."

Garrison replies, "I don't know what you're talking about."

Collins stops him, "Mr. Garrison, don't bullshit us. We know what you did, we can prove it, and unless you start cooperating, you'll get the needle."

Beeks, "I have to say that even if you do cooperate, you could get the needle. Mass murder is serious business."

Collins, "My partner here is concerned about where the bomb came from, but I care more about who paid you and convinced you to do it. If Calvin Crane isn't behind this, who is?" She pauses and gives him a 'you're caught' look. "Try to imagine a needle in your arm."

He collapses and admits, "It was John Wilson."

FBI agents escort Garrison in handcuffs out to the street, through a crowd of protestors and reporters, to a waiting SUV. Beeks is stunned by the development that the attack was perpetrated by President Wilson, "Well, we're certainly in over our heads now."

Collins looks at him like he's a rookie, "You know he's lying. Wilson never planned this."

Beeks tells her, "We still need to interview the President, and right now. This story is going to break big."

Collins, "Well Garrison sure didn't deny Calvin Crane's involvement. But if it wasn't President Wilson, who the hell is he protecting?"

In the Oval Office, the President and Governor Crane are still negotiating, "the bottom line, Susan, is that I can't do it. The American Presidency is far too important to be bargained nor negotiated. It is not a pawn, and neither am I. I don't know how or why this all began, but we will get to the bottom of it, I promise you."

She is ruthless, "Well, according to our investigative services, it seems clear that you hired Skip Garrison to arrange for the bombing of the Capitol. Once everyone learns that, they will side with me."

"That is a lie and the press would never believe it."

Susan stands up and walks out of the Oval Office, "Too late Mr. Former President."

She passes an aide who walks in and whispers something to the President. The President tells the aide, "Turn it on." The Aide turns on the TV.

Stanley Ropert is reporting the breaking news. 'America: The Civil War' appears on the bottom of the screen, "As we continue our live continuous coverage of "America: The Civil War", we bring you these live shots of noted Washington DC attorney Skip Garrison being arrested at his downtown office."

The President tells his aide, "Get Hunter on the phone."

"Yes sir, Mr. President. FBI agent Collins and NSA agent Beeks are here to see you."

"Show them in."

In a Las Vegas hotel suite that is set up like a military command center, General Baxter is on the phone, "Calvin, what did your wife say."

"She met with Wilson and he said no. Prepare to launch against the east coast immediately."

Beeks and Collins enter the Oval Office. The President stands with his back to them staring out the window at the Rose Garden.

He tells them, "Come in. Andrew I thought you were with the CIA?"

"Good morning Sir. I've been officially transferred to the NSA due to this domestic issue. I legally can't work this investigation while at the CIA."

The President, "I hope you're not torturing anybody."

Beeks doesn't say a word.

The President asks, "How we doing? What's the status of the investigation?"

Collins, "We assume you heard about Skip Garrison's arrest."

Beeks, "That was us, Sir."

Collins gives Beeks a 'shut up' look.

The President offers, "You know he was my classmate at Yale."

Beeks, "We know, Sir."

Collins, "That's what we want to speak to you about."

"Sure. Sit down." They do. The President continues, "We went to Yale together, Law school, fraternity, the whole thing."

Collins inquires, "What about Calvin Crane, did you know him at Yale?"

"Yeah, we were all in law school together. Do you think he's involved?

Beeks, "We can't say for certain, but it's possible."

The President, "Well let's not ignore the elephant in the middle of the Oval Office. Do you suspect me?"

Beeks, "Garrison fingered you."

"What? Why would he do that?"

Collins offers an explanation, "We don't know yet, but we think he's full of crap. We think he's protecting someone in addition to Calvin Crane. They apparently think framing you strengthens their cause."

Howard Mellon's mansion is enormous – it is like combining the Titanic and the White House. Guests arrive as bodyguards with machine guns stand spread throughout the grounds. The driveway is over a mile long and there are several helicopters on the front lawn from which men in beautiful traditional white Arab attire exit. They are surrounded by their own bodyguards.

In a sitting room, Susan, Calvin, and Howard Mellon sit quietly while Calvin is on the phone, "Very good General Baxter." As he hangs up the phone, "Baxter will attack Washington tomorrow."

Mellon turns to Susan, "Well then it's time to make good on your threat Susan"

She suggests, "Maybe I should call Wilson again."

She picks up the phone, but Mellon demands, "Put the phone down. Nobody is calling anyone."

Susan explains, "I didn't think it was a 'take it or leave it' offer. I thought we were negotiating."

Mellon tells Calvin, "Can't you control your wife?"

"I don't need controlling."

Calvin, "Honey, you need to understand."

Susan interrupts him, "Shut up Calvin."

Mellon reflects, "She doesn't know, does she? You never told her."

"Told me what?"

Mellon reveals the truth, "Skip Garrison wasn't hired by Wilson. Your husband hired him."

"What?"

"Tell her Calvin."

Susan yells, "What did you do?"

Mellon, "Tell her. She already knows or she should if she's smart. The real question is, does the President know that she knows?"

Susan is visually upset, and says to her husband in a stricken voice, "Some of our closest friends were in that building."

Mellon interrupts, "They were casualties of war."

Calvin stands up and pours himself a scotch as Susan raises her voice, "Calvin, you better say something, god-dammit. We're all going to jail for murder."

Calvin ignores her as Mellon explains, "Nobody is going to jail. This has nothing to do with crime. It has to do with politics and patriotism. We are putting America first. The United States killed hundreds of thousands, maybe even millions, in Iraq and the Middle East and do you think any American will ever be charged with war crimes? In the meantime, we killed that son of a bitch Saddam Hussein and convinced world leaders that he had committed war crimes –

and at the same time, convinced most Americans that he was the one who attacked us on 9/11."

Several Mellon bodyguards knock and enter the room and stand in front of the only door, blocking it. Mellon continues, "You see my dear, whoever controls the media, the propaganda machine, as it's sometimes negatively called, controls the world."

One of Mellon's men says, "Mr. Mellon, Prince Ali has arrived."

He concludes, "This is not the first time we've had to take drastic measures to maintain our freedom and the American way of life."

Susan asks, "And what way is that Howard?"

"It's my way." Mellon stands up and walks towards the door where his men are standing post. More bodyguards walk in.

Calvin tells Susan, "Sweetie, I was gonna tell you."

Mellon, "You are a part of history, both of you. That's because I create history. But don't forget that I can also re-write it. Susan, if you don't screw this up, you may just become the first woman President of the United States. Think of it, it's hard to believe that the first female vice president will not be a Democrat. Like I said, I create history."

Another bodyguard enters and says, "Mr. Mellon, General Baxter is on the phone for you."

Mellon instructs his men, "Our guests will be staying here with us for a little while. Please make sure they are safe and not disturbed by anyone. They need some time to think and to grow up."

"Yes sir," his men reply, and address Susan and Calvin, "We're going to need your cell phones."

As Mellon leaves the room, "The two of you, get your shit together." His men close the door and walk toward Susan and Calvin, who meekly hand over their cell phones.

"Governor Crane, please stand-up so we can search you."

Humiliated, she does.

At the White House, Secret Service agents, police officers, and soldiers are standing post. Many have machine guns drawn. German shepherds are barking. Tanks and armored vehicles are stationed in front of the gates. American soldiers continue to arrive by the truck-load.

In the Oval Office, Beeks asks the President, "What about the other guys you went to school with?"

Collins adds, "Besides you, who else was close with both Garrison and Calvin Crane?"

The President, "Nobody."

Beeks, "Come on, don't bullshit us. We know someone else has to be involved pulling the strings."

Surprised by his language, the President gives him a look of shock - so does Collins.

"Andrew Mellon," says the President.

Beeks asks, "Who is he?"

"He's the heir to the Mellon fortune," Collins responds. "Oil, gas, steel, shipping."

Beeks, "Why would he be involved?"

Collins nods her head in the affirmative, "Because..."

"Because his family, along with another hundred or so industrialists and financiers, control the Republican Party," interrupts the President. "They call themselves conservatives, though they're really not. They don't give a damn about illegal immigration, gun control, or gay marriage. They take those positions to appeal to voters. At the end of the day, they want lower taxes for their friends, less government oversight over their businesses, and control of the world economy."

Collins, "Well I wouldn't have put it like that."

"Mellon is very dangerous," the President adds, "and if he is behind this, and he knows you can prove it, you'll never find him and your lives are in grave danger."

Beeks, "We probably can prove it, given enough time."

Wilson expresses great frustration, "We've run out of time. I'm about to be framed by Susan Crane for blowing up the Capitol – and the press is playing right into their hands."

THE WHITE HOUSE

The world looks on anxiously as the siege on Washington DC is imminent. Worldwide, stock markets are in shambles. For the first time since the tragedy at the Capitol, the sun can't be seen this morning. The clouds gather as Confederate soldiers armed with tanks and Humvees race toward the Potomac. General Baxter stands on the street next to his jeep looking like General George Patton, cheering on his troops as they march by.

The radio reports, "At dawn in Washington DC, our lead story is that talks between Governor Crane and President Wilson have reportedly broken down, and that Confederate forces are less than ten miles from the Potomac River, ready to cross into Washington DC."

In the sky Confederate F-15s fly toward Washington preparing to attack. At the same time, inside the Operations Center at the NMCC, Major O'Connor hangs up the phone and reports to Fitzgerald and Hunter, "The Pentagon is secure. We have several thousand troops in the city with two divisions coming in tonight from North Carolina. They will be able to counter attack in the morning if we lose the city. We will engage the F-15s in thirty seconds."

In the airspace above Washington D.C. Super Hornets under Hunter's command are flying over the Potomac preparing to engage Confederate F-15s.

"Sir, do we have permission to engage?" the Hornet Commander asks NMCC.

"That's affirmative, Commander."

Hornet Commander, "F-15 Eagle commander, this is the US Air Force, please identify yourself. You have entered secured air space. Divert now."

No response.

"Please identify yourself or we will engage. Again, divert now."

No response.

Hornet Commander, "OK gentlemen. Prepare to engage. Lock on targets - fire."

The Hornets fire. The missiles move toward the F-15s. Several are hit. The F-15s fire back. The Hornets greatly outnumber the F-15s. One F-15 gets through and is heading toward the White House.

NMCC on the radio, "One got through. One got through Commander."

"I see him. I got tone. Fire three."

The Commander's Hornet fires and hits the F-15. It crashes on the Washington Mall as the Hornet flies over the Washington Monument.

Everyone cheers at NMCC as Major O'Connor, Hunter, and Fitzgerald watch the camera view of the Hornet as it flies over the Mall. But then an alarm sounds. "What's that?" asks O'Connor.

A Sergeant responds, "Enemy F-15s forty miles outside of mid-town Manhattan."

Fitzgerald asks, "How many?"

Sergeant, "Over twenty-five."

Hunter screams, "Scramble two more squadrons of Hornets from Teterboro now!"

In the New York City airspace, Confederate F-15s are flying toward Manhattan as Hunter's Hornets take off.

A Lieutenant in the cockpit of the lead Hornet hears his instructions over the radio, "This is NMCC, you have about twenty-five F-15s twenty miles south of the city - permission to engage."

The Hornet Lieutenant, "That's affirmative."

The Hornets and the F-15s are flying right toward one another.

F-15 Commander, "Red team lock on targets and prepare to fire." His weapons systems screen shows the Empire State building as the target, "Fire."

The F-15s fire their missiles. The missiles hit their targets in lower Manhattan -- one missile hits the Empire State Building.

At NMCC, Major O'Connor informs Hunter, "The Empire State Building was just hit."

Hornet Lieutenant, "Fire." The Hornets fire and most of the F-15s are hit. The remaining F-15s fly away.

At the Potomac River, the only bridge still standing is the Arlington Memorial Bridge. General Baxter is on the Virginia side in between the river and Arlington National Cemetery while the American soldiers are on the other at the western tip of the Washington Mall surrounding the Lincoln Memorial. An aide approaches Baxter who stands right outside his Humvee, "Our F-15s in New York are retreating south."

Baxter asks, "What did they hit?"

His aide, "Lower Manhattan is on fire and we hit the Empire State building."

In Manhattan, people are running through the streets just like on 9/11. On CNN Stanley Ropert sits in the anchor chair, "You are looking at live shots from lower Manhattan. As you can see, there is wide-spread destruction"

At The White House, Secret Service agents rush past the President's secretary and into the Oval Office. Hunter's top SEAL commander, Colonel Tanner, enters the room as the agents surround the President. Everyone watches CNN, replaying over and over again, people running for their lives on the streets of New York and the Empire State Building on fire.

Colonel Tanner, "Mr. President, Chairman Hunter has ordered your immediate evacuation. Please come with us."

"I'm not leaving."

"Sir, General Baxter is only miles away." Tanner insists, "We have no more time."

"If I leave, the next picture will be Susan Crane sitting in this chair on TV establishing presidential policy. I'm staying."

Tanner speaks into his radio, "NMCC command, this is Colonel Tanner with the President. He is a no go. Repeat he is a no go. Please advise."

At NMCC Hunter asks, "What did he say?"

Standing next to him, Major O'Connor repeats, "He says President Wilson is staying."

"All right," Hunter responds. "Move the 53rd Rangers from the Capitol to sixteen hundred. Get the chopper ready and tell The President that I'll be there in five minutes."

As Hunter begins running out, Beeks shouts, "Wait!" Hunter stops. "I'm coming too."

"So am I," adds Collins as they all run out toward the waiting chopper.

Lower Manhattan is on fire. In midtown, people race out of the Empire State Building as Stanley Ropert continues to report on the attack. "As we watch these incredible images from Manhattan, we have received an unconfirmed report that President Wilson is being investigated by the FBI for the bombing of the Capitol. Sources at the conservative American Values Council have issued a statement substantiating these findings."

At the Potomac River, Baxter's Confederate troops are being engaged by American soldiers. The Americans are overwhelmed by Baxter's tanks. The Confederates cross the river, securing the other side passing several destroyed tanks and dead American soldiers.

As Hunter's chopper lands on the White House grounds, Secret Service agents guard every door to the White House. American soldiers and tanks have surrounded the White House with guns pointed toward the Potomac. One mile from the White House, Confederate troops are only a few blocks away from the Washington Monument.

Hunter, Beeks and Collins head to the Oval Office to brief the President. As they speak among themselves Collins, "We're convinced it was Skip Garrison and Calvin Crane, probably backed by Andrew Mellon."

"Andrew Mellon is one of the richest men in America," says the President, "Why would he be involved?"

"Greed, narcissism, power – what's the difference?" replies Beeks.

Collins asks, "The question is how involved was Governor Crane?"

"What do you think?" Hunter counters.

"From a legal point of view we don't need to flip Crane to make our case. From a non-legal point of view, it's not my place to provide political advice."

Hunter, "Beeks, I know, you can't hold your opinion back."

"She probably knew after the fact," he answers. "My sense is that her husband and his old pal Mellon were manipulating her. Garrison was just the operative to procure the bomb and get it into the Capitol where it could do the most damage."

Collins adds, "The bottom line is motive, and these guys and their parents and grandparents before them have been manipulating politics and the US government since World War II; Cuba, Kennedy in Dallas, Nixon and the break-in, Iran Contra, Monica Lewinsky and Ken Starr, the Iraq War, Trump and Russia. The only difference is that this time they got caught. Or we will catch them soon enough."

As they reach the door to the Oval Office, Hunter concludes, "Here and now, we have a civil war threatening our nation's future, and here and now, we need to stop it. Then we'll get Calvin, Mellon and everyone else who played a role in this disaster."

Hunter, Beeks and Collins enter. The President is sitting at his desk surrounded by Secret Service agents with additional agents covering the exits. Hunter instructs Beeks and Collins, "Just get the correct story out there in the media as quickly as possible. If they blame the President and it sticks, we're all finished."

The President overhears what Hunter is saying, "What about the media?"

He responds, "We've definitely proven that two of your fellow Yalies are behind this and are also responsible for the bombing of the Capitol. Beeks and Collins can prove it. But if the wrong story gets out there, you're done."

"How can you be sure?"

"Look who's behind the blackmail," Hunter suggests.

Collins ads, "Only the blackmailer could really know what and how it happened."

The President is shocked, "Governor Susan Crane?

Hunter, "She's the only one who is blackmailing you to accept her conditions."

The President asks, "But why?"

Just then a massive explosion over the parks and gardens somewhere near the Washington Monument can be seen through the windows. Secret Service agents shield the President. Just outside the Oval Office, soldiers, police officers and Secret Service agents run south toward the southern gates, the Ellipse, and the Washington Monument.

On CNN, Stanley Ropert is in the anchor chair, "This just in - Governor Crane's Confederate troops are now only a mile from the White House."

In the CNN control room, producer Kelly is on the phone, "All right Rob, let's go live. Interrupt Stanley. Just start – speak!"

Rob Black, "I'm moving through the White House, and can see that Confederate forces led by General Baxter have reached the Washington Mall." Explosions echo throughout the city as he continues, "The President is still inside the Oval Office protected by Secret Service agents."

In the Oval Office an agent says, "Sir, we have to move now!"

Hunter adds, "Mr. President, we need to move you to a secure location immediately. We can evacuate you now. Sir, we need to maintain a working government."

Beeks adds, "Sir, Collins is on the phone with the networks right now. Her proof will break the case wide open, but we need you to still be alive or their coup d'etat will succeed."

Collins on the phone, "Yes, Kelly. That's right. He was framed. I'm texting you the proof right now."

Kelly asks Collins, "Is Governor Crane a suspect?"

Collins responds, "She is more than a suspect. She will be arrested for conspiracy and we are also issuing arrest warrants for her husband and for Howard Mellon. We believe Mellon bank-rolled the whole thing, or at least that's where the evidence points."

For the next two hours, Rob Black at the White House, and Stanley Ropert at CNN headquarters, in Atlanta broadcasted the only live coverage of the attack on the White House. It was like 1991, all over again when Bernard Shaw, Peter Arnett, and John Holliman were the only journalists reporting live from Baghdad at the beginning of the first Gulf War. The other networks had either been cut off or were reporting that the Confederated States could prove to the world that President Wilson was guilty. A civil war had begun and they were reporting that if the President were to step down, the country could unite. Some reports suggested that the President had been captured and that clemency had been offered in exchange for resigning. However, one person was standing all alone on the Truman Balcony of the White House overlooking the South Lawn – Rob Black.

At CNN, Kelly's team gets her attention when it is quite clear that all the channels are carrying the CNN feed. The monitors broadcasting live pictures from within the White House are all from Rob's cell phone.

"I can see him now in the distance -- General Baxter is standing in front of his mechanized units. I can even see some tanks. The American soldiers seem to be withdrawing behind the White House itself. Wow, did you just see that? It was like a giant flashbang. We are lit up by flood lights. I think they're coming."

He continues, "Can you hear that gunfire? Now we're hearing a lot of gunfire. Small arms fire, but a lot. Alright, they are moving. General Baxter is leading his troops toward the White House. Those were definitely explosions on the South Lawn. Oh my God, that explosion must have killed 30 secret service agents. Baxter's tanks have just blown through the outer perimeter and it looks like the soldiers are entering the White House grounds. The agents are withdrawing back to the West Wing. They are completely overpowered. There seems to be a pause now in the gunfire. I've gotta move."

Stanley, "Be careful there Rob. Get someplace safe. I will just recap that this is live video of a Confederate battalion of mechanized and armored units. In some of this video it looks like the battalion has split in two -- half flanking left and the other to the right. Most importantly, according to our sources, and contradictory to what most other news outlets are saying, we can confirm that the President has not been captured"

"I'm back Stanley. Can you hear me?"

"Yes, go ahead Rob. What do you see?"

"I had to move away from the railing but I'm still outside. The entire second floor here seems to be empty. But I still see agents all around. I can see the Oval Office. I have to move closer. Can you see this? I can look through the glass and see – I'll show you. There are many agents and marine guards surrounding the West Wing. There are also many agents outside the Oval Office. Their guns are all out. It looks like they are taking up defensive positions."

In the Oval Office, everyone has their guns drawn. Senior military officers enter the room with brief cases, including the "football" with the nuclear codes.

Collins hangs up the phone and nods to Hunter who says, "Mr. President, it's time."

As the President rises from his chair and moves toward the doors, a missile hits the Oval Office. It explodes but the bullet-proof glass does not shatter. The Secret Service agents jump on the President to protect him. Collins draws her gun. So does Hunter. The agents move the President out of the Oval Office as Colonel Tanner leads the way into the adjacent reception area.

On the South Lawn outside the West Wing, Secret Service agents have their machine guns drawn. As Baxter's Confederate troops approach them, they are quickly overpowered.

Rob continues reporting from the Truman Balcony, "I can see the remaining agents running for cover back into the West Wing. There are some on the roof of the West Wing. Confederate troops are heading toward me now, still firing on the agents. The President appears to be trapped between the Oval Office and the Cabinet Room. I can see flashes from the Cabinet Room."

Stanley, "Are Confederate troops in the West Wing? Rob, are you still there?"

Rob, "I can't move and I must stay quiet. The troops have entered the White House and are outside on the West Colonnade and in the Briefing Room firing on those last agents protecting the President. It cannot be long now as Confederate soldiers are converging from three sides – from the South Lawn, from across the Rose Garden and now from the north where the press offices are. Something is happening now. I can see the President through the windows. Can you see that? This may be it. The President may be forced to surrender at any moment."

Just then a fresh team of Secret Service agents exit from the Oval Office and begin firing on the Confederate forces. Unfortunately they too are outnumbered. Hunter sees this and bursts out of one of the glass doors shooting at Baxter's men and shouting to the few remaining agents, "Get the President out of here right now."

The agents, headed by Colonel Tanner and Collins, move the President from the secretary's office into the hallway. They are quickly met by Baxter and his Confederate troops who fire on them from the other end of the hall. A shot is fired. Tanner is down. The Secret Service agents grab the President and push him back into the secretary's office. Collins gets off several shots before grabbing Tanner and taking cover behind the door.

Hunter, "What happening?"

"Four men at the end of the corridor," Collins responds. "I think one of them is Baxter."

While still firing through the open door at Confederate troops in the Rose Garden, Hunter looks down at Tanner, "Is he okay?"

"He will be," responds one of the agents.

Hunter, "You need to get out of here now. I can't hold these guys off forever."

Beeks draws his gun and joins Hunter at the door. Collins tells the agents, "All right you are with me. We'll clear the hall. If we don't get the President through that hall and out of the lobby quickly, we're all dead." The agents and Collins enter the hallway shooting at Baxter and his men. With adrenaline pumping, they enter the hallway killing the Confederate soldiers at the other end. "Hunter, we're clear let's go."

Collins and the agents run down the hallway but within a few steps, they are again under Confederate fire. The agents take cover back in the secretary's office to protect the President.

On CNN Stanley Ropert is reporting. "Rob, I don't know if you can hear me? Can you hear me, Rob? Okay we seem to have lost him so I will recap. What we know now is that the White House is under attack by Confederate soldiers and that Secret Service agents are trying to evacuate the President. We have been able to see and hear the incredible explosions coming from the West Wing. We understand that the President wanted to stay at the White House against the advice of the military and Secret Service, and that it may too late for an evacuation. Confederate troops outnumber the

Secret Service agents, and we believe that the President may be trapped in the halls of the White House."

In the hall just outside the Cabinet Room, Secret Service agents are shooting at the Confederate soldiers. Collins and Beeks also fire in a barrage but the soldiers return fire, hitting some agents. From the secretary's office, one of the Secret Service agents hands Hunter a Rocket Propelled Grenade. Hunter quickly jumps in front of the cross fire and fires it. A large explosion kills all the Confederate soldiers in the hallway, including Baxter, and in the process, takes out the wall behind them. Before the smoke even begins to clear, Hunter orders, "Move the President out to the car."

"Evac everyone now," Beeks shouts. The agents run out through the hole in the wall surrounding the President who moves with them.

In the CNN control room, producer Kelly is typing on her computer while on the phone and tells her team, "All right, we're going with this breaking news." Pointing to her computer, she tells the Assistant Director, "Tell Stanley to read this - now."

Secret Service agents and American soldiers are protecting the north-western driveway. The President exits the West Wing surrounded by agents led by Collins, "Let's go, let's go. Get him in!" Once the President is rushed into a black SUV it speeds off with other Secret Service SUVs and police cars exiting the grounds, still taking fire from the remaining Confederate soldiers.

In the newsroom, Kelly is drinking coffee pacing back and forth in front of her monitor. Her Assistant Director is becoming more and more nervous as Kelly asks, "Are we going to get this to Stanley or should I..."

"Three seconds. OK. Go."

Kelly, "Stanley, go – read it,"

On worldwide live TV, he unprofessionally asks Kelly, "Are you sure?"

"Yes God dammit. Read it now!"

He begins, "CNN has confirmed that the report issued by the American Family Council an hour ago and broadcast on all major conservative news outlets, is false. We understand that the Director of the FBI and their key investigative team will hold a press conference outlining their evidence and we will join them live in about fifteen minutes. In the meantime, we have received confirmation from several federal officials that there is strong evidence that previous reports that the bombing at the Capital was orchestrated by President Wilson are false. I repeat, those reports appear to be false. In fact, we expect the announcement by the FBI to confirm that the bombing of the Capitol was the first stage of a coup d'état planned by one of the wealthiest men in the world, Pittsburgh steel tycoon Howard Mellon."

Within the hour, FBI agents, SWAT teams, and police officers approach the Mellon Mansion. Armored vehicles move toward the house. Several armed henchmen loyal to

Mellon are protecting the front door. Using silencers, the agents and SWAT team fire at Mellon's men and kill them.

The images on CNN show Mellon and several aides being escorted out of the house by FBI agents. Stanley reports, "A federal arrest warrant has been issued for Howard Mellon. Arrest warrants have also been issued for Governor Susan Crane and her husband Calvin Crane."

One Month Later

President Wilson is at his desk when Hunter enters the room and stands in front of him.

"Good morning, Jimmy."

"Good morning Mr. President."

"Good to see you again and well. So where are we?"

"We rounded them all up: Calvin Crane, Howard Mellon, even General Baxter may pull through. The Attorney General told me that grand jury indictments will be handed down before the end of the day -- for murder, treason and espionage – the works."

"And what of the others?"

"Who would that be?" asks Hunter.

"The millions who went along with them, who wanted to divide the Union."

"For what? What was their crime?" Hunter thinks for a moment and then adds, "What did Lincoln do one-hundred and fifty years ago? Didn't he allow all of them, Union and Confederate alike, to go back to their families?"

"What happened to Robert E. Lee, although only a general, and The Confederate President then were radically different"

Hunter, "Almost no one even knows the name Jefferson Davis."

"Ironic, isn't it? History teaches us that Lee had not only accepted the loss in the South, but did more to encourage southerners to move on than Lincoln could have ever done."

"Meanwhile, Davis lived in denial after prison and ultimately died a lonely man."

The President, "I spoke with the new Speaker of the House this morning. The House and the Senate are committed to reuniting the country. The American people need healing and so I spoke with him about the VP post."

Hunter asks, "Was he interested?"

"I didn't ask him. I told him that I would be picking a leader and not a politician." The President rises from his chair and walks around his desk to Hunter. He reaches out his hand. "You interested?"

"I serve at your pleasure, Mr. President," as they shake hands.

One Year Later

At FBI Headquarters Collins is on the phone when Beeks walks in. "Yes sir, I'll tell him. He just walked in. Thank you, sir. Good night." She hangs up the phone.

"Who was that?"

"The President."

Beeks looks surprised, "So you speak to him directly now."

"It's unbelievable."

"What?"

"How jealous you are."

"I'm not jealous."

"First you definitely are jealous. Second, you were thinking that you were going to spend the night with me."

"What? Who? Me?"

"Yeah, I know how you think – and you're right. You are going to spend the night."

"Really?"

"We're going to the State of the Union. Then the President wants us on a plane to the Middle East tomorrow morning to track more missing nuclear materials. The satellite got a fix on two possible locations in the Persian Gulf. The SEAL team will meet us at Andrews tomorrow morning."

She puts on her coat, "Flights at Oh-four-hundred. Try not to be late."

"I'm not getting up that early."

"You're not getting up at all. We're working all night. You can sleep on the plane."

He's standing at the door. It's open. She walks toward him and says "By the way, what did Hunter say about me?"

"He said beware – she's smarter than you."

"What a nice compliment. Let's pick up dinner on the way. What do you want, McDonalds or Burger King."

He looks at her like she's crazy, "You're kidding right?"

"Don't worry. I'll get burgers from Burger King and fries from McDonalds."

At the White House, the door to the Oval Office opens and in walks Henry Johnson, the Secretary of Education. President Wilson is sitting at his desk, looking relaxed and relieved that the crisis of the Civil War has been averted, and the nation is again united. He is enjoying a fine cigar, "Hank, come in." He rises and walks over to Johnson and shakes his hand.

"Good evening, Mr. President."

"As you know, a cabinet member is normally asked to remain in the Oval Office during the speech, but since we're doing the State of the Union from the White House tonight, I think it would be best if you were at the Pentagon."

Johnson looks nervous, "That sounds fine to me, sir."

"Don't worry – everything is going to be fine."

Covering the event on CNN from his anchor chair is Stanley Ropert. "We have been informed by the White House that security has been especially tight for the past three days in preparation for the President's State of the Union Address. And of course, given the events of one year ago, no one is surprised. We now go to White House correspondent Rob Black who is there."

Rob, "Here at 1600 Pennsylvania Avenue, several tents have been erected creating one large tent on the South Lawn. It is large enough to hold one thousand people. Security is obviously very tight, with everyone walking through metal detectors and there are Secret Service agents everywhere, along with more members of the media than I ever remember being assembled here at the White House"

Stanley, "The President is only seconds away and the crowd has become quiet -- here he comes."

The doors to the White House are closed, and Secret Service agents stand post on either side. The doors open and several more agents exit the White House followed by the President. They enter the tent following the Crier, "Here ye, here ye. Mr. Speaker, the President of the United States."

The President enters. Everyone rises and applauds. He begins...

EPILOGUE

*A*lmost everywhere we look, the story is the same. In Latin America, in Africa, in Asia, in the councils of the world and in the jungles of far-off nations, there is now renewed confidence in our country and our convictions.

For this country is moving and it must not stop. It cannot stop. For this is a time for courage and a time for challenge. Neither conformity nor complacency will do. Neither the fanatics nor the faint-hearted are needed. And our duty as a party is not to our party alone, but to the Nation, and, indeed, to all mankind. Our duty is not merely the preservation of political power but the preservation of peace and freedom.

So let us not be petty when our cause is so great. Let us not quarrel amongst ourselves when our Nation's future is at stake. Let us stand together with renewed confidence in our cause − united in our heritage of the past and our Hopes for the future − and determine that this land we love shall lead all mankind into new frontiers of peace and abundance.

Remarks intended for delivery to the Texas Democratic State Committee in the Municipal Auditorium in Austin, Texas by President John F. Kennedy. November 22, 1963.